MW01174760

THE REASON FOR THE PELICAN

NEW EDITION

JOHN CIARDI

DRAWINGS BY DOMINIC CATALANO

AFTERWORD BY X. J. KENNEDY

For Gary, 1997

[signature]

WORDSONG
BOYDS MILLS PRESS

Published by Wordsong
Boyds Mills Press, Inc.
A Highlights Company
815 Church Street
Honesdale, Pennsylvania 18431
Printed in the United States of America

Publisher Cataloging-in-Publication Data
Ciardi, John.
   The reason for the pelican : new edition / by John Ciardi; drawings by
Dominic Catalano.
[64]p. : ill. ; cm.
Originally published by J.B. Lippincott Co., N.Y., 1959, with illustrations by
Madeleine Gekiere.
Afterword by X.J. Kennedy.
Summary : Thirty-fifth anniversary edition of John Ciardi's first book of poetry
for children; newly illustrated.
ISBN 1-56397-370-7
1. Children's poetry, American. [1. American poetry.] I. Catalano, Dominic, ill.
II. Title.
811.54—dc20   1994
Library of Congress Catalog Card Number 93-61163

"The Principal Part of a Python" © 1955, "The Reason for the Pelican"
© 1955, "Rain Sizes" © 1959, and "There Once Was an Owl" © 1959 by the
Curtis Publishing Co.

Book designed by Tim Gillner
The text of this book is set in 13-point New Caledonia.
The drawings are done in pencil.
Distributed by St. Martin's Press

10 9 8 7 6 5 4 3 2 1

To Myra
and to everyone
with an imagination
that tickles

By John Ciardi

CONTENTS

To all the children who read this book:

When I was a little girl, I was having trouble learning to read. I was very lucky, though, because my father wrote these poems to help me. He thought I would have fun with the words and rhymes, and learn to read at the same time. Well, I did learn to read. And now I share these poems with my children. I hope you will enjoy them, and maybe you could pick your favorite one and read it out loud to someone you love.

Myra Ciardi
October 1994

THE REASON FOR THE PELICAN

The reason for the pelican
Is difficult to see:
His beak is clearly larger
Than there's any need to be.

It's not to bail a boat with—
He doesn't own a boat.
Yet everywhere he takes himself
He has that beak to tote.

It's not to keep his wife in—
His wife has got one, too.
It's not a scoop for eating soup.
It's not an extra shoe.

It isn't quite for anything.
And yet you realize
It's really quite a splendid beak
In quite a splendid size.

RAIN SIZES

Rain comes in various sizes.
Some rain is as small as a mist.
It tickles your face with surprises,
And tingles as if you'd been kissed.

Some rain is the size of a sprinkle
And doesn't put out all the sun.
You can see the drops sparkle and twinkle,
And a rainbow comes out when it's done.

Some rain is as big as a nickle
And comes with a crash and a hiss.
It comes down too heavy to tickle.
It's more like a splash than a kiss.

When it rains the right size and you're wrapped in
Your rainclothes, it's fun out of doors.
But run home before you get trapped in
The big rain that rattles and roars.

THE BUGLE-BILLED BAZOO

The noisiest bird that ever grew
Is the Bugle-Billed Bazoo.
(He's even noisier than YOU.)

He starts his YAMMERING as soon
As he's awake, then SHOUTS till noon.

Then SCREAMS from noon till six or so,
And then he YELLS an hour or two.

He's not like other birds who sing
Because the flowers are out for Spring.

He SHRIEKS and SCOLDS the whole day through
Just to be heard. If you do, too,
YOU'RE a Bugle-Billed Bazoo.

SOMEONE

There was a boy just one year old
What he said I haven't been told.

There was another and he was two.
He said to the first, "I'm older than you!"

"Ha!" said his sister, who was half-past three.
"Call *that* old? Just look at me!"

Someone has a birthday and then he's four.
Then he has another and he isn't any more.

Now for a question—Look alive:
How old is Someone? He just turned . . .

If Someone's five, how long does it last?
And how old is he when it's past?

You can't save the numbers. Time plays tricks.
How old is Someone? He just turned . . . .

Where *do* the birthdays go? Good Heavens!
All the Sixes have turned to . . . .

Someone Seven has a year to wait
And when it's over Someone is . . . .

What's after Eight? That's right! And then?
Right again: Eight . . . Nine . . . and . . . . !

WHAT YOU WILL LEARN
ABOUT THE BROBINYAK

The Brobinyak has Dragon Eyes
And a tail the shape of a Fern
And teeth about Banana Size,
As one day you may learn
If ever you sail across the Sea
On the Shell of a Giant Clam
And come to the Forest of Foofenzee
In the Land of the Pshah of Psham.

There is no language he can't speak
And you may, if you please,
Be swallowed whole in French or Greek,
Or nibbled in Chinese.

And once inside the Brobinyak
You'll meet a lot of friends:

The Three-Toed Gleep and the Saginsack
And a covey of Two-Tailed Bends.

The Russian Bear is always there,
      And Glocks from the Polar Sea.
And Radio Eels with static squeals,
      And the Piebald Peccary.
The Splinterwave from his Ocean Cave
      Will greet you at the door.
And the Green Kilkenny collect your penny
      And pitch it along the floor.
The Banjo Tern and the Fiddling Hern
      Will play you a Wedding March.

But keep your eye on the Lullaby
     Or he'll nibble your collar for starch.
Oh keep your eye on the Lullaby
     And never speak to the Mullet,
Or the Scrawny Shank will leave his Tank
     And nibble you quick as a bullet.
And never look at the Seven-Nosed Hook
     Or, with a frightful roar,
He'll sniff enough of his Pepper Snuff
     To sneeze you out the door.

Oh the Brobinyak has Dragon Eyes
And a tail the shape of a Fern
And teeth about Banana Size,
As one day you may learn
If ever you sail across the Sea
On the Shell of a Giant Clam
And come to the Forest of Foofenzee
In the Land of the Pshah of Psham.

THE PINWHEEL'S SONG

Seven around the moon go up
    (Light the fuse and away we go)
Two in silver and two in red
And two in blue, and one went dead.
    Six around the moon.

Six around the moon go up,
    Six around the moon.
Whirl in silver, whirl in blue,
Sparkle in red, and one burned through.
    Five around the moon.

Five around the moon go up
    (Rocketing up to the moon)
Sparkle and shine in a wonderful flare,
Till one went dead a mile in the air.
    Four around the moon.

Four to rocket around the moon.
    (Look at the crowds below!)
Four gone zooming above the sea,
But one got lost, and that makes three.
    Three around the moon.

Three around the moon go up.
    (Don't bump into a star!)
Silver and Red and whistling loud,
But Blue crashed into a thundercloud.
    Two around the moon.

Two around the moon, well, well.
    Two to reach the moon.
But Silver turned left, and Red turned right,
And CRASH! they splattered all over the night
    Falling away from the moon.

None of them going as far as the moon?
     None of them going that far?
Quick! Somebody light me another fuse.
But I'm all burned out . . . it's just no use . . . .
     It's really
         too far
            to
               the
                   moo . . . .

THERE ONCE WAS AN OWL

There once was an Owl perched on a shed.
Fifty years later the Owl was dead.

Some say mice are in the corn.
Some say kittens are being born.

Some say a kitten becomes a cat.
Mice are likely to know about that.

Some cats are scratchy, some are not.
Corn grows best when it's damp and hot.

Fifty times fifty years go by.
Corn keeps best when it's cool and dry.

Fifty times fifty and one by one
Night begins when day is done.

Owl on the shed, cat in the clover,
Mice in the corn—it all starts over.

HOW WOODROW GOT HIS DINNER

Woodrow sailed across the sea
—I don't know where he went—
But on the way he came upon
A girl named Millicent.

He found her on an island
In the middle of the sea,
Because of water all around
And nowhere else to be.

She married him in church one day
Because the church was near,
And she took him home for dinner
Because he called her Dear.

Had Woodrow stayed at home I think
He wouldn't have gone to sea,
And he wouldn't have had his dinner
—But perhaps you won't agree.

THE SAGINSACK

The Saginsack has Radio Horns
　　　And Aerials for ears,
And judging by his grin, I'd say
　　　There's something that he hears
That rather tickles him, although
　　　He'll never tell you what
Because the Needlewing has sewn
　　　His mouth—which keeps it shut.

He may be hearing the Brobinyak
　　　(On record, I suppose)
Asleep in the shade of an Everglade
　　　And snoring through his nose.

It may be that he's listening
　　　To the Wife of the Man in the Moon,
Or the Razor Fish in his shaving dish
　　　Whistling a chanty tune.

Or even perhaps (by short wave)
　　　The Dog Star barking away
At the Swivel Tail Comet that shines on the Summit
　　　Of Mars in a kittenish way.

He may be hearing the Goldfish
　　　In the bowl by the window sill
Talking of Home in the Golden Foam
　　　As homesick Goldfish will.

He could be listening to YOU
　　　(A rather frightening thought.)
It could be anything at all—
　　　The Saginsack won't say what.

He may (perhaps you've guessed it)
    Be listening to the breeze
That blows from the lair of the Fan Tail Bear
    High up in the Pyrenees.

(A wonderful breeze, I've heard it said,
    All full of Spanish singing
And Warbler's calls and Waterfalls
    And Early Bluebells ringing.)

He may be listening, some say,
    To mice at play in the attic.
And others say it's all a fraud
    And that all he hears is static.

Some say he's listening for the sound
    The Baker's Wagon makes.
(He always buys a bushel of pies
    And a tubful of chocolate cakes.)

He could be hearing yesterday
    And everything you thought,
And grinning away as if to say,
    "I know, but I won't tell what."

Whatever he hears, whatever he thinks
    He keeps it under his hat.
And though I've tried and listened and spied
    I can only tell you that

The Saginsack has Radio Horns
    And Aerials for ears,
And judging by his Grin, I'd say
    There's something that he hears
That rather tickles him, although
    He'll never tell you what
Because the Needlewing has sewn
    His mouth—which keeps it shut.

SEVEN SHARP PROPELLER BLADES

Seven sharp propeller blades
Boring through a cloud
Leave seven silver tunnels,
And then they're very proud.

Seven little oysters
Digging just offshore
Leave seven silver bubbles
On the ocean floor.

Seven sharp propeller blades
Fly apart and fall
On seven silver bubbles,
Shattering them all.

Blow another bubble,
Place your bets.
Ready oysters?
Here come the jets.

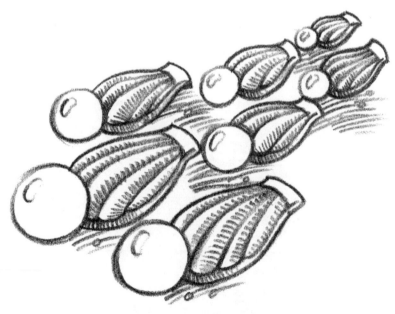

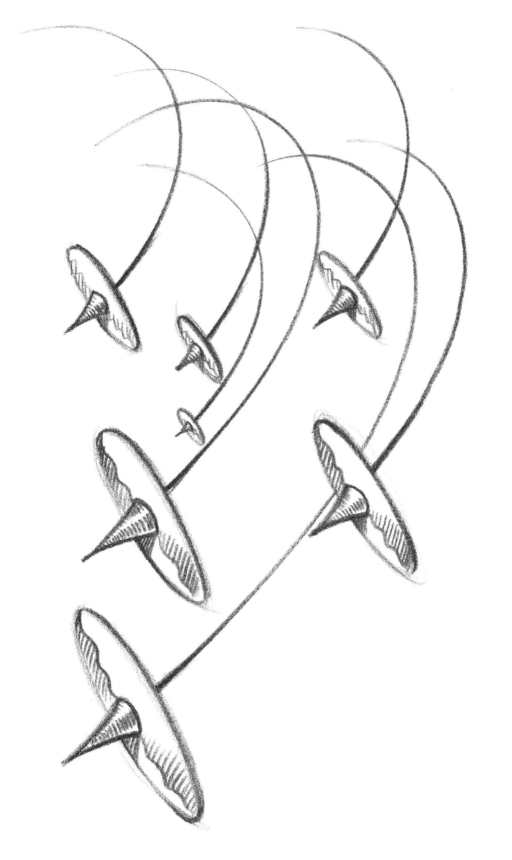

HALLOWEEN

Ruth says Apples have learned to bob.
Bob says Pumpkins have a job.
       Here's the man from the Witching Tree.
       Ask *him* since you won't ask me:
Do you think Ruth is telling the truth?

"Man from the Tree, your skin is green.
What night is this?" "It's Halloween."

Ruth, Ruth, you told the truth.
The man says Apples *have* learned to bob.
The man says Pumpkins *do* have a job.
The man come down from the Witching Tree
Says he wants someone. No, not me.
Says he wants someone good and true—
       YOU!

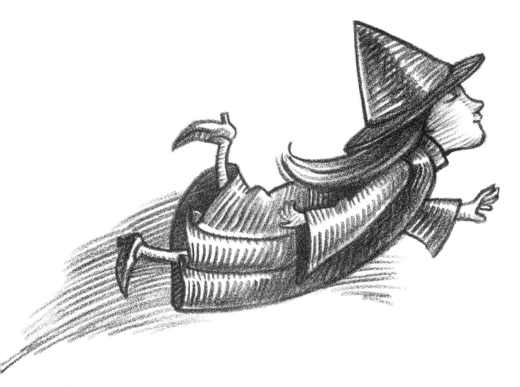

Mother, Mother, Ruth's gone flying!
Hush, children, stop that crying.

Mother, Mother, she's up in The Tree!
Climb up and tell me what you see.

Mother, she's higher than I can climb!
She'll be back by breakfast time.

Mother, what if she's gone for good?
She'll have to make do with witches' food.

Mother, what do witches eat?
Milk and potatoes and YOU, my sweet.

SAMUEL SILVERNOSE SLIPPERYSIDE

Samuel Silvernose Slipperyside
Lived on an Iceberg high and wide.
He slept all night in his Iceberg Cave,
And he fished all day in the Silver Wave,
And he carried his catch through the Crystal Floes
Carefully balanced on his Nose,
And he sang as he hurried to and fro,
And he never caught cold at Forty Below.

And all the Seals from Nome to the Pole
Said, "There's a good one, 'pon my soul!
He catches more fish in a day
Than all the young ones in the Bay.
And there's not another in all the Floes
Has such a Silver Balancing-Nose."

In fact, the neighborhood pointed with pride
To Samuel Silvernose Slipperyside.

Samuel Silvernose Slipperyside
Heard them talk and swelled inside.
"As soon as Spring comes round," said he,
"I'm off across the Silver Sea.
Everybody says I'm good:
The place for me is Hollywood.
There I will balance Canes and Cats
Rubber Balls and Baseball Bats
Vinegar Bottles and Tall Silk Hats
Eels and Lamps and Shoes with Spats,
All on my Silvery Nose."

So Spring came round and the Whales came North
And Samuel Silvernose sailed forth.

"You'll be sorry you ever left home,"
Said Wise Old Seals from the Pole to Nome.
"You'll be sorry, 'pon my soul,"
Said Wise Old Seals from Nome to the Pole.
"You'll wish you had your Iceberg Cave
When the Sea Lion jumps from the Silver Wave."

Samuel looked across the sea
And shook his head. "I can't agree.
Icebergs are no place for me."

And so he shed his winter coat
And hitched a tow from a Whaling Boat
As far as Bristol Bay, then took
A steamer out around the Hook,
And down the coast to Aberdeen,
And then a Tug Boat painted green.

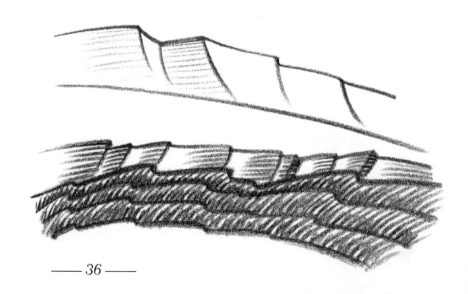

"This is more like it," Samuel cried,
"Sailing along on the ocean wide.
Towed along on a Silver Wave."
And he thought of home and his Iceberg Cave
And of what the Wise Old Seals had said,
And laughed and laughed and shook his head.

He passed a school of Silver Fish
And scooped them up in a Seaweed Dish.

He passed a school of Corkscrew Eels
(The favorite food of traveling Seals)
And he caught enough for a dozen meals.

And laughing and feeding and feeling brave
He sang all day to the Silver Wave,
Until they came to the Sea Lion's Cave,
And saw the Sea Lion on the shore,
And heard the Sea Lion roar.

"Here's where I leave you!" cried the Wave,
And hid in the rocks by the Sea Lion's Cave.

"Swim for your life!" said the Morning Tide.
"I'll swim faster!" the Sea Lion cried.
And some say Samuel replied,
But I understand from the Morning Tide
That long before he *might* have replied,
Samuel Silvernose Slipperyside
Was being worn by the Lion—inside.

And Wise Old Seals from Nome to the Pole
Said, "I knew it, 'pon my soul!"
Wise Old Seals from the Pole to Nome
Shook their heads and said, "Stay to home!"
Whenever a Seal with a Silver Nose
Balanced his catch through the Silver Floes.

And right or wrong, it's bad for a Seal
To be the Sea Lion's morning meal.

Which wouldn't have happened, except for Pride,
To Samuel Silvernose Slipperyside.

PRATTLE

How old is thirty-six, about?
Or twenty-twelve? Or fifty-two?
Is it longer away than I can shout?
Daddy, is it as old as you?

Is forty much? When I'm nine or more
Will I be scratchy enough to shave?
How old do you have to be before
It's not much trouble to behave?

I know the end of the world. It's where
You go in a ship and it's all hunched out
With nothing but ocean. Can I go there
When I'm big as twenty-five, about?

LUCIFER LEVERETT LIGHTNINGBUG

Lucifer Leverett Lightningbug
Was born inside a broken jug
On the Fourth of July, or slightly before
At twenty-seven minutes to four.
And it wasn't but an hour or so
Before he began to glow and glow.

He didn't even wait till dark
To have the first try at his spark.
He glowed and glowed and glowed in the grass
And glowed and glowed all night—alas!

"For to glow all night when you're one day old
Is proof," said he, "that you're bright and bold."
And Lucifer Leverett glowed away
As if he would glow till Judgment Day.

A gray old firefly stopped to say,
"Glow too hard and you'll glow away.
Better go easy on the tinder
Or you'll be nothing but a cinder."

Said Lucifer, "Sir, you may be right,
But oh, what a lovely, lovely light!"
And he glowed and he glowed and he glowed away,
As if he would glow till Judgment Day.

Said wise old fireflies watching him glow,
"I wonder does his mother know
What Lucifer Leverett is about.
She ought to come and put him out,
Or he'll be frizzled clean away
Long before the break of day."

Lucifer Leverett laughed outright
And danced on the grass and sang all night,
"Oh what a lovely, lovely light!"

And sure enough, by the break of day
Lucifer Leverett frizzled away.
He glowed so hard for one so small
That by dawn he had charred to nothing at all.

He glowed so hard that he glowed right through.
—As very likely you would, too,
If you had a glow like a firefly
The night before the Fourth of July.

And the moral, very sad to say,
Is: "Glow too hard and you'll glow away."

THE PRINCIPAL PART
OF A PYTHON

The principal part of a python—
As any one plainly can see—
Is the part that begins in the middle
And goes both ways indefinitely.

The trouble is, no one can tell you
Whether it's tail, sir, or nose.
It simply begins in the middle
And grows and grows and grows.

I think the Python might like it
If someone who knows could decide
When he wriggles along through the jungle
Which end is getting the ride.

Is it tail that is doing the pushing
Wherever the Python goes?
Or does tail just hang there resting
While he wriggles along on his nose?

Don't *you* think the Python might like it
If someone who knows would decide
When he wriggles along through the jungle
Which end is getting the ride?

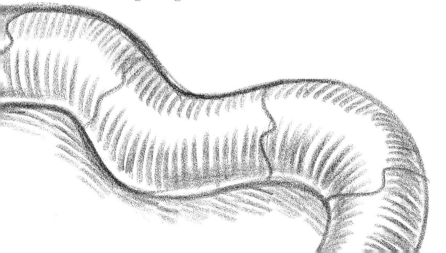

THIS IS I AT WORK AT MY DESK

This is I at work at my desk
Making another rhyme.
I do it just for practice—
A jingle at a time.

I have a shelf all full of books
And a cage of Radio Eels.
I tune them in on the Brobinyak
Or chop them up for meals.

But even though I eat my eels
Like sausage—link by link—
I love them and I'm not the sort
Of person you might think.

It isn't done because I'm cruel—
I eat them with a tear,
Because I've nothing else to eat
And meat is very dear.

I sit then at my desk and work
And weep for what I've done.
But when I finish with this rhyme
I'll eat another one.

But it won't be done because I'm cruel—
I do it with a tear,
Because I've nothing else to eat
And meat is very dear.

THE ARMY HORSE AND THE ARMY JEEP

"Where do you go when you go to sleep?"
Said the Army Horse to the Army Jeep.
"Do you dream of pastures beside a creek
With meadow grass to make you sleek?
Do you dream of oats and straw in a stall
And never a load in the world to haul?
Do you dream of jumping over the wall
To get at the apples that fall in the Fall?
Do you dream of haystacks steeple-tall?
Or what do you dream if you dream at all?"

> "Rrrrrrrrr," said the Jeep
> And "Chug!"

"I dream of being greased for a week
On the Happy Rack by Gasoline Creek
In the Happy Garage where there's never a squeak,
But lakes of oil so black and sleek,
And Spark Plug Bushes, and no valves leak.
That's where I go when I go to sleep,"
To the Army Horse said the Army Jeep.

> And "Rrrrrrrrr," said the Jeep
> And "Aaaaaaaaaa!"

I TOOK A BOW AND ARROW

I took a bow and arrow
(I don't know where I got it.
I may have found it somewhere.
Perhaps I even bought it.)

However it was, I took it
And shot it straight and true
At a Polar Bear in Washington Square
And hit a policeman's shoe.

Some say it was the left shoe.
Some say it was the right.
Some say it wasn't a Polar Bear
But a Cinnamon Yak dyed white.

It really doesn't matter,
But I *know* it was a Bear:
Whoever saw a Cinnamon Yak
In the middle of Washington Square!

THE HERON

The Heron has two wooden legs.
Perhaps you won't agree,
But if you met him on the street,
He'd tell you openly.

He'll say Goodmorning bright and loud
As the Alderman or the Mayor.
And sing you a song of The Rainbow Cloud
And the Giant Bobo's Lair.

He'll tell you about the Kalakegs
That sail in Teacup Ships.
But never ask about his legs
Or he'll snip off your lips.

Some say he had legs just like yours
Till he sailed to fight the Kilts,
But when he came home from those wars
He hobbled back on stilts.

Some say it was at Ararat,
And some at Bengal Bay.
But never ask the Heron *that*:
He's crotchety that way.

He'll tell you yarns of Tiger Eggs,
And how snakes got their hips.
But don't you ask about his legs
Or he'll peck you on the lips.

THE RIVER IS A PIECE OF SKY

From the top of a bridge
The river below
Is a piece of sky—
        Until you throw
        A penny in
        Or a cockleshell
        Or a pebble or two
        Or a bicycle bell
        Or a cobblestone
        Or a fat man's cane—
And then you can see
It's a river again.

The difference you'll see
When you drop your penny:
The river has splashes,
The sky hasn't any.

I SOMETIMES THINK ABOUT DOLLAR BILLS

I sometimes think when I'm alone
  It would be very strange
Should I become a dollar bill
  And meet myself in change.

I think it would be rather hard—
  Considering the times—
To leave myself in pennies
  And meet myself in dimes.

The hardest part of it would be—
  As you well realize—
That when I met myself, I'd be
  Hard to recognize.

WHY NOBODY PETS THE LION AT THE ZOO

The morning that the world began
The Lion growled a growl at Man.

And I suspect the Lion might
(If he'd been closer) have tried a bite.

I think that's as it ought to be
And not as it was taught to me.

I think the Lion has a right
To growl a growl and bite a bite.

And if the Lion bothered Adam,
He should have growled right back at 'im.

The way to treat a Lion right
Is growl for growl and bite for bite.

True, the Lion is better fit
For biting than for being bit.

But if you look him in the eye
You'll find the Lion's rather shy.

He really wants someone to pet him.
The trouble is: his teeth won't let him.

He has a heart of gold beneath
But the Lion just can't trust his teeth.

HOW TO TELL THE TOP OF A HILL

The top of a hill
Is not until
The bottom is below.
And you have to stop
When you reach the top
For there's no more UP to go.

To make it plain
Let me explain:
The one *most* reason why
You have to stop
When you reach the top—is:
The next step up is sky.

AFTERWORD:
JOHN CIARDI'S 'BIG RAIN THAT RATTLES AND ROARS'

The unpretentious book that lies before you offers, first of all, a way to regale children. It crackles with energy, overflows with rich word-music, and dishes up square meals for the imagination. Besides, having been out of print and unobtainable for years, it now has a certain historical interest. It is the first children's book written by John Ciardi (1916-1986), poet and critic, editor and broadcaster, teacher and scholar, and translator of Dante's *Divine Comedy*.

Strange though it now seems, when Ciardi brought out *The Reason for the Pelican* in 1959, writing poems for children was a pursuit far less respectable than it has become today. In the world of American poetry beyond the world of children's books, for a poet to address kids was thought slightly disreputable, something that a really good poet wouldn't do. Oh, writing for children was deemed permissible for a light-versifier like Ogden Nash. And it is true that, here and there, elder poets such as Robert Frost, Langston Hughes, and E. E. Cummings had printed a scattering of children's poems; defying convention, Elizabeth Coatsworth and David McCord had produced volumes. But among serious poets of Ciardi's generation, it wasn't usual to publish a children's book—not if the poets wished to maintain their status among their peers. Only the irrepressible William Jay Smith had dared do so before Ciardi; a few years later, other leading poets like Randall Jarrell, Theodore Roethke, May Swenson, and Richard Wilbur would also turn out children's books and win acclaim for them. Because of their distinguished examples, perhaps also because of a recent tendency to take children's literature seriously, it is now possible for a poet to publish a collection of children's verse without being exiled from the literary republic.

John Ciardi, I believe, was responsible to a large extent for this change in climate. He had a down-to-earth, democratic attitude toward poetry: he thought it could encompass any subject matter and ought to appeal to everybody. In person, he didn't fit the stereotype of the sensitive poet clutching a lily in his medieval hand. When I first saw him in the late 1950s, he looked to me like a burly Italian American grocer with a kind but no-nonsense eye, who might size you up and see if you were a good credit risk. He held in contempt anyone who regarded poetry as some sort of delicate hothouse hibiscus. He liked feelingful, intelligent, well-made poems free of emotional slush, moral equivocation, or mental slither. You can tell he did from his hard-hitting *Selected Poems*, especially from the long autobiographical work "Lives of X." Ciardi placed great stress on reading poetry aloud, and in all his work, for both children and adults, you can practically hear his distinctive deep, gravelly voice boom through—a voice that goes straight to the point.

Although sympathetic and large-minded as a critic, Ciardi could be tough when necessary. As poetry editor of the *Saturday Review*, he outraged scores of his readers by reviewing and panning the poems of Anne Morrow Lindbergh. (Many canceled their subscriptions, but Ciardi stuck to his guns.) As a teacher of verse writing, he had only a limited patience with blatherers. Sometimes he would draw a horizontal line across a student's poem at the point where he had become bored and stopped reading, and often it was very early in the unlucky poem that his merciless blue pencil fell. A poet has a duty to *interest* us, Ciardi believed; a poem in its opening lines must persuade us to sign a "sympathetic contract" and go on reading. A despiser of cant, Ciardi once wrote a postscript to his *Who's Who* biography to the effect that anyone who looks back on his own career is already a has-been. (This note jangled harshly against the self-congratulatory notes and Polonius-like advice of other biographees.) He once told me that he'd long wanted to put together an anthology of poems that he wouldn't be ashamed to hand to a teenaged boy, and I am sorry he never got around to it.

As you might expect, in his approach to child readers and listeners, Ciardi is about as far as you can get from those Victorian American pedagogues (some of them still practicing) who assume that poetry for children has to be reassuring and cute; who seem to say, "Here, my teeny-weeny man or woman, is a poem-lollypop for you." That just isn't John Ciardi's style. He knew that kids are living people, like the rest of us, with feelings and resentments, people who fall down and get dirty and occasionally punch one another in the snoot. He enlarged the permissible scope of children's verse, and I suspect he helped make it possible for Shel Silverstein, Jack Prelutsky, and other later children's bards to be a little more disconcerting and outrageous than their predecessors.

In his poems Ciardi likes to display real kids and actual, fallible families. He shows us things unreal and absurd and preposterous, too, which he knew would be dear to kids' hearts. Critics, he told a correspondent, have rendered our view of poetry overly intellectual—"but the kids have a fresh eye." When in 1982 the National Council of Teachers of English surveyed children's taste in poetry, 422 respondents in the upper elementary grades picked Ciardi's "Mummy Slept Late and Daddy Fixed Breakfast" as their favorite poem out of 113 poems in the running. I suspect that this triumph must have delighted Ciardi more than if he had won a Pulitzer Prize.

I believe that the work of John Ciardi has had a strong and lasting impact. Ciardi threw open the musty old parlor of American children's verse, with its smell of rose petals and camphor, and he let in a blast of fresh air. He swept away a clutter of nineteenth-century poetic diction. He altered the way we look at poetry for children, helping us see it as a fun-filled romp instead of a saccharine pill or a dose of propriety. He addressed himself to actual twentieth-century American kids with all their faults, kids who (as this book notes) sometimes prattle on at a great rate about nothing much, or taunt younger siblings with their own superiority. With his prodigious energy, Ciardi left a large and substantial body of work for children—a baker's dozen of books, not counting still more that have appeared posthumously—and all the while carried on several other careers as adult poet, TV and radio broadcaster, sometime professor and magazine columnist, traveling lecturer, and (toward the end of his life) a maker of personal dictionaries that bespeak his love for words.

In some of the poems in *The Reason for the Pelican*, Ciardi harks back to a familiar vein of classic nonsense. His fantastic creatures—the Brobinyak, the Saginsack—recall Lewis Carroll's Jabberwocky, while his lonely and unfortunate hermit, Samuel Silvernose Slipperyside, may be cousin to the doomed, eccentric bachelors of Edward Lear. This strain of old-fangled nonsense isn't Ciardi's most characteristic and original note, but it is beautifully sounded indeed. No one will want to draw a horizontal line across any of the poems in this collection and quit reading. Ciardi keeps waking us up, sometimes with insults: the Bugle-Billed Bazoo is "even noisier than YOU." And the reader may be agreeably surprised by a poem's unexpected turning:

Mother, what do witches eat?
Milk and potatoes and YOU, my sweet.

Now, that isn't the way a conventional children's poem used to go. And children's poetry hasn't been the same ever after.

I don't know anyone else who has written a greater quantity of satisfying verse for children. Several of the items in this book ought to stick around for as long as English is decipherable. In particular, I'd finger for probable immortality such deft things as "Rain Sizes," "Someone," "Halloween," "The Principal Part of a Python," "The River Is a Piece of Sky," "How to Tell the Top of a Hill"—but I'm only guessing, to be sure. Anyhow, let me salute John Ciardi and his deathless pelican, whose splendor is its own reason for being, and congratulate the publisher on making this wonderful book once again available to those bright and fortunate children of today who refuse to spend all their free time looking at television.

X. J. Kennedy
October 1994